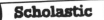

# The Magic School Bus®
## GETS ANTS IN ITS PANTS™
### A Book About Ants

Scholastic Inc.

New York   Toronto   London   Auckland   Sydney

Based on the episode from the animated TV series
produced by Scholastic Productions, Inc.
Based on *The Magic School Bus* book series
written by Joanna Cole and illustrated by Bruce Degen.

*TV tie-in book adaptation by Linda Ward Beech and illustrated by John Speirs.*
*TV script written by Jocelyn Stevenson, Kristin Laskas-Martin, and Brian Meehl.*

ISBN 0-590-40024-X

12 11 10 9 8 7 6 5 4          6 7 8 9/9 0 1/0

Printed in the U.S.A.                    23

First Scholastic printing, February 1996

You never know who's going to show up for a visit to Ms. Frizzle's class. Take the other morning, when Keesha arrived. She was following a tiny guest. "Meet my friend the ant. Isn't she amazing? I wonder where she's headed?" asked Keesha.

"This is no time for *antics*," said Carlos. "We've got to pick a project for the science fair."

The Friz was tossing things from the closet. "Ah, the passion of science," we heard her say. "Where is...? Oh, there it is!"

The Friz put something on her head. It seemed to be a pair of antennae. She looked like our visitor.

In the meantime, Keesha had lost her ant. Arnold found her on his Mallow-Blaster cookie.

"So that's why she came in here," said Keesha. "She was looking for food."

Then Keesha got an idea. "Maybe we could do something about my ant for the science fair," she said.

"Well," said Dorothy Ann, "according to my research, where you find one ant, there are usually more nearby."

"That's right, Dorothy Ann," agreed Ms. Frizzle. "Ants live together in nests."

"But what could we *do* with ants?" asked Phoebe.

Keesha looked at Liz. The class lizard was holding a video camera.

"That's it!" yelled Keesha. "We'll make a *movie*."

Phoebe shook her head. "At my old school, lizards weren't allowed to make movies," she said.

My ant is a natural star.

This whole thing seems unnatural to me.

"I'll write it," offered Carlos.

Phoebe wanted to help Carlos. Keesha would be the director, and her ant would be the star. The rest of us would play ants. Liz, it seemed, would do the filming. And Ms. Frizzle would take care of costumes.

It'll be about an ant with a long nose called Eleph*ant*.

Groan!

Just as Keesha began to give orders, her ant ran out of the room. We all followed.

Keesha's ant soon caught up with lots of other ants.

"Look at them all!" exclaimed Keesha. "How do I know which one is mine? I've lost my star!"

Dorothy Ann had a book about ants. "According to my research, your star has been telling the other ants about Arnold's cookie," she explained.

"Excellent observation, Dorothy Ann. Ants don't really talk," said the Friz, "but they *do* communicate."

The Friz told us that a food-finding ant is a forager ant.

"I've got it!" shouted Ralphie. "We'll make a western starring an ant that rounds up food."

"We can call it *Food Dude*," said Carlos.

Oh, no! I'm getting that shrinking feeling again!

Very observ*ant*, Arnold.

All of a sudden, Ms. Frizzle got that look she sometimes gets. Then the Magic School Bus honked.

"All aboard," Ms. Frizzle said.

We each found a seat and fastened our safety belts. It's good to be prepared when you're going on a field trip with Ms. Frizzle. *Anything* can happen.

Soon the bus was spinning and shrinking. When it stopped, the bus looked like Arnold's cookie. It tasted like it, too. But where were we?

"Different ants do different jobs," explained Ms. Frizzle. "Remember the forager ants that find food?"

Suddenly, the bus was lifted up.

"Hey, we're being foraged!" cried Wanda.

"Keesha, is the movie going to star a forager ant?" Phoebe asked.

"And are we going to costar as food?" Arnold added. He sounded nervous.

"No," said Keesha.

The bus landed with a thud.

"Where are we?" asked Dorothy Ann.

"We're on location," said Ms. Frizzle.

Keesha looked out the window. "It's an anthill!" she called.

"It's perfect. We'll meet the ants up close and personal. Come on, Liz."

Liz and Keesha left the bus — but not for long! Hundreds of giant ants came after them.

"Who let them on the set?" yelled Keesha.

"They look like they're guarding the nest," said Phoebe.

"Great!" said Ralphie. "The movie can star a guard ant."

Ralphie said, "It'll be perfect for the wide screen with stereo sound and..."

"Smell-o-vision," said the Friz.

We had no idea what the Friz was talking about.

"Guard ants use their antennae to smell if we're friend or foe," she told us. "Ants don't understand words, but they do understand smells."

I hope we smell friendly.

The ants began to smell us.

"The ants are checking to see if we smell like them," explained the Friz. "Their bodies make scented chemicals called *pheromones*." With that, she pushed a handle on the bus and sprayed us!

"Now we smell like these ants," said the Friz. "So the guard ants will let us into the nest."

She led us from the bus. "As I always say, class, when visiting a nest, smell like the rest."

The guard ants checked us with their antennae. They wanted to be sure we were friendly. Then we entered the tunnel to their nest.

"Hey, look at this!" yelled Tim. He pointed to hundreds of ants running back and forth. The place was crawling with them.

Excellent! A cast of thousands!

It must be rush hour!

"Okay, places everyone!" yelled Keesha in her best movie director's voice.

But we weren't quite sure how to act like ants.

"What about makeup, Keesha?" asked Dorothy Ann.

"And what's the plot? Who's the star?" asked Carlos.

"Maybe we should get to know the ants better," Phoebe suggested.

"Good idea, Phoebe," said the Friz. "Understanding begins with observation," she told us.

We're not going inside an ant, are we?

"I love it!" cried Keesha. "See the ant, feel the ant, be the ant."
We watched some ants in action.

"This ant's rubbing its head, and this one is licking itself,"
said Phoebe.

"They're cleaning themselves," Tim figured out.
We saw two ants passing food from mouth to mouth.

One of the ants gave a sticky blob to Arnold. He knew what it was right away — part of his cookie. "Oh, sure, give it back to me *after* you've chewed it," Arnold grumbled.

But a movie about ants sharing food didn't seem very exciting.

Carlos crossed that idea off his list. "Okay," he said. "This movie isn't going to be about a forager ant, a guard ant, or a food-carrying ant."

That's not how we pass food in my house.

Keesha was still looking for a star for our movie. As she walked toward one of the tunnels, some ants grabbed her and raced away. Then some other ants picked up the rest of us. Now things were getting very exciting! We were part of a great chase scene!

Suddenly, they dumped us in front of a chamber.

"Wait a minute!" yelled Tim. "What's in there?" He pointed into a room where ants were carrying something.

"They're like little worms," observed Dorothy Ann.

An ant gave one to Arnold.

"You look like you're holding a baby," said Dorothy Ann. "Maybe it's a baby ant."

Ms. Frizzle explained that baby ants are called larvae. Just one was a larva. And that's what Arnold was holding.

"Who ever heard of a movie about larvae?" asked Keesha.
We watched the ants move the larvae.
"I'll bet they're trying to keep the larvae warm," said Tim.
Ms. Frizzle explained that these were nurse ants. "Their job is to move the young around the nest to keep them the right temperature. When they get a little older the larvae will become pupae."

Rock-a-bye, baby, everyone cares.
When the air cools, they move you upstairs.

But Keesha didn't want to do a movie about a larva or a pupa. "Where's the excitement?" she asked.

"What about an egg?" asked Phoebe. "Where do ant eggs come from anyway?"

"Good question, Phoebe," said Ms. Frizzle. "The eggs came from the queen!"

Keesha loved it. "That's it — a royal star!" she cried.

Does the queen have servants?

Carlos and Keesha began to look for the queen. While they were looking, Phoebe noticed water coming through the walls.

"Heads down!" called the Friz. The nest started to shake and the tunnel caved in.

As we picked ourselves up, ants ran past us. There were ants everywhere. "Look!" yelled Tim. "They're already repairing the nest!"

"That's right," said Ms. Frizzle. "They're builder ants."

Maybe they can build the sets for our movie.

Keesha was still on a mission. "To the queen!" she shouted. "There's only one and she's our star."

At first we didn't even see her.

"There she is," said the Friz. "She's the biggest one."

"But she's not doing anything," said Wanda.

Ms. Frizzle said the queen was the only ant who laid eggs.

Keesha was upset. "The queen laid an egg. The end," she said. "I thought a movie about ants would be perfect for our science project. But I was wrong!" She turned and ran out of the nest.

Do we have to bow?

Does she have an agent?

Phoebe found Keesha sitting in the rain.

"No movie, no story, no star," Keesha said sadly. "What kind of star just sits there and lays eggs?"

"Without the queen, there wouldn't be eggs," Phoebe said.

"So," said Keesha, "without the ants that bring food, there wouldn't be a queen."

Suddenly, she and Phoebe understood. All the ants worked together. Without the forager ants, there wouldn't be food. Without the builder ants, there wouldn't be a nest. Without the guard ants, the nest would be attacked.

Without me, there wouldn't be a movie.

Wow! It's a survival movie!

Keesha and Phoebe ran toward the bus. "They're all stars!" exclaimed Keesha. "Every ant in an anthill has a job to do. Just like we each have a job to make this movie."

"Forget the movie!" said Arnold. "There's a mud slide!"

"It will wipe out the anthill," Keesha said. She spotted a magnifying glass on the ground.

"Action!" yelled the Friz.

We grabbed the magnifying glass to block the mud. We saved the nest just in time!

Back at school, our science movie was a big success. We each had a different part, and the movie couldn't have been made without everyone's help!

## Some More Antics

**Producer:** Okay, Liz, we'll let everyone know how much work you did on the movie.

*Rrrrrring.*

**Producer:** Hello?

**Caller:** You work on the Magic School Bus, right?

**Producer:** Er, I'm just one of many who work on it.

**Caller:** Well, an ant colony has thousands of ants, but I only counted 137 in your show.

**Producer:** Oh, you must be an account*ant*! Ha, ha! Well, you're right. There are thousands of ants in one nest. But we couldn't afford to hire that many extras.

**Caller:** There are also thousands of different *kinds* of ants. You only showed one kind.

**Producer:** Right. There are ten thousand different kinds of ants.

**Caller:** You didn't say anything about all the ants in the movie being female.

**Producer:** Right again. Almost every ant in a colony is female. The only thing males do is mate with the queen. You know, you're pretty smart.

**Caller:** Actually, I'm brilli*ant*!

**Producer:** That's it. One more call. Hello, Magic School Bus.

**Second Caller:** This is the Academy Awards returning your call.

**Producer:** I have a question about the rules. Is it possible to nominate a lizard for best camera work?

# At the Anthill
## A Project for Parents and Kids

You know that ants live and work together. You also know that they share food. What foods do ants like? Try this to find out.

1.   Locate an anthill.

2.   Fill several jar lids with different foods. Try using honey, salt, maple syrup, and flour.

3.   Place the lids in a circle about one yard from the anthill.

4.   Try to answer these questions:
   • How long does it take the ants to find the food?
   • Which food or foods do the ants seem to like best?
   • What do you notice about the way the ants travel to the food?
   • How do you think the ants tell one another about the food?